Traveling Again, Dad?

Traveling Again, Dad?

Written by Michael Lorelli
Illustrated by Drew Struzan

Publisher's Cataloging-in-Publication Data
Lorelli, Michael –
    Traveling Again, Dad? / Written by Michael Lorelli; illustrated by Drew Struzan. -- Darien, Conn.: Awesome Books, LLC., c1996.
        p.   col. ill.   cm.
    SUMMARY: A lighthearted picture book for ages two to teens that provides suggestions on how a family can make a parent's work-related travel into an educational experience for the loved ones left behind.
    ISBN: 0-9646302-0-6

1. Work and family – Juvenile literature. 2. Business travel – Juvenile literature. 3. Children of working parents – Juvenile literature. I. Struzan, Drew – II. Title
HD4904.25.L67   1996   306.85 dc-20   95-60604

PUBLISHERS DESIGN SERVICE
121 E. Front St., Suite 401
Traverse City, MI 49684

Publishers
Design Service

Printed in Hong Kong

10 9 8 7 6 5 4 3 2 1

To Karen and Elizabeth

I'm so glad,

I got to be your dad.

Love,

Daddo

Traveling Again, Dad?

Hi. My name is Awesome. I'm the head hamster here and this is a picture of my family. There's Karen and Bethy and their Mom and Dad.

We're all a little sad, 'cause Dad needs to go away for a whole week.

We had a great dinner——my personal
favorite——pizza crumbs, the night
before Dad left on his trip. We all noticed
Dad's packed suitcase by the door.

My car isn't nearly as fast as Dad's,
  but I don't need to travel too far, either.

When I drive or skate under the table to catch a little dinner, Bethy and Karen pretend they're not feeding me.

I think Mom and Dad know that they feed me. Pizza sure is better than those little green pellets they put in my cage!

I'm going to miss you Dad. I wish you weren't going away.

Dad explained that being away from the family now and then was part of his job. Lots of moms and dads have to travel for work.

Dad left the next morning.
He said he'd miss all of us.
Even me!

Bethy thought about Dad's trip while she was in school. We all miss him when he's gone. Me too!

Dad thought about us when he was in his meetings. Too bad we have to be apart for a whole week.

I wonder if anyone thinks of <u>me</u> when they are away.

The map on the refrigerator helps us to keep track of Dad's travels.

This week he's in Philadelphia. Some people call it Philly.

I was reminded of my favorite song.

♫ Philly Philly ♫♪ ♫ Bo Billy Banana

Bana Bo Bana ♪ ♫ Fe Fi Fo Philly ♪ ♫ Philly ♪

Mom said, "Let's send Dad a note at his hotel." "How can we do that?" asked Bethy and Karen.

"You'll see," said Mom. "We'll go to the drugstore where they can send it right away, and he'll get it tonight on a fax machine."

Bethy dreamed of Dad returning home in a few days, so they could all play softball together.

Maybe we can all play. I'll play shortstop and our cat, Blinker, can play third base.

"Mom, Dad's home!" Karen shouted.

"Hi Dudes", Dad said excitedly. "It's so great to be home. I can't wait to tell you all about my trip. Let's go inside, OK?"

"It's hard to be away from you guys," said Dad. "But it's always great to get home to all of you..."

"And that's Awesome..."

Special thanks to two people without whose efforts, this book would still be in the idea phase.

The first is Dylan Struzan, the illustrator's wife, who through her creativity, sense of humor and sensitivity transformed the original script into a movie-in-a-book. She and Drew are a wonderfully complementary couple to whom I am grateful beyond words.

Secondly, I want to acknowledge John Taylor, from Taylor, Dougherty & Partners, Inc., who acted as our production advisor and graphic designer, and in the process enlarged the creative vision of the book.

Both individuals believed in the cause and were happy to donate their time.

Michael Lorelli